arnaud rykner

I Will Not Come

translated by
sue boswell

THIS IS A SNUGGLY BOOK

Original title: *Je ne viendrai pas*
Original publisher: © Actes Sud, 2000
Translation Copyright © 2022 by Sue Boswell
All rights reserved.

ISBN: 978-1-64525-112-5

ARNAUD RYKNER is a writer and academic. He has published eight novels, several of which have appeared in paperback including *Le Wagon* which won the Jean d'Heurs prize for historical fiction in 2011. He is a Professor and Director of Research at the Sorbonne Nouvelle in Paris, and has also authored a dozen essays and edited many collected works. As a theatrical producer he has notably put on the works of Nathalie Sarraute, Maurice Maeterlinck and Bernard-Marie Koltès. He is a Visiting Professor at Rutgers University and a Senior Research Fellow of the University of Durham.

SUE BOSWELL studied French Language and Literature at UCL and for a time taught French at Goldsmiths University of London. She then moved into university administration, specialising in external relations and communications. Later she became a translator for the Wiener Holocaust Library, and translated Arnaud Rykner's novel *Le Wagon* as *The Last Train* (Snuggly Books, 2020). Her other translations include Marcel Schwob's *The Assassins and other Stories*, Ilarie Voronca's *The Confession of a False Soul* and with her husband, Colin Boswell, Gustave Kahn's *The Mad King*, also for Snuggly Books.

I Will Not Come

Who, if I cried out, would hear me among the Angelic Orders? And even if one were to suddenly take me to its heart, I would vanish into its stronger existence.

Rainer Maria Rilke

PART ONE

I

THE first time they came I wasn't expecting them.

They come into my bedroom, first one, then two, then three, up to one thousand and one as in the tales. Unbearable. Then they leave.

Time passes. A day. A month. Maybe more.

An angel comes in, slowly, gently, his eyes on mine. He approaches, silently. Coming close to me, a few metres away, he shouts. Without opening his mouth, he shouts.

It seems he isn't doing anything, but I know that he's screaming.

A cry from far away, a cry that I recognise, long, piercing and silent.

I cover my ears but the angel screams more loudly, without moving, with his lips closed.

I'd rather he kept quiet. I try to soothe him. My angel, my little angel, stop screaming, at least open your mouth. But the angel keeps screaming, stubbornly. Blood is running from my ears, making a pool between him and me. He looks at his reflection in the pool. Then, satisfied, he leaves. (He could at least have mopped up.)

What funny ideas these angels have. That's what I've been constantly repeating to myself since then. Each time they came.

And they who knew must have been saying to themselves that they had definitely made a bad choice.

II

STILL more time passes. Too much time. Then an angel comes in. And then a man I don't know.

The man comes in facing the angel.

The man looks at the angel.

They look at each other in the same way that the angels looked at me that first time.

Suddenly the angel screams. Still that same silly scream you can't hear. He screams and the man collapses. Then the angel comes up to him. He kneels and cradles the man. Pietà.

Then another man comes in. He sees the man and the angel. The pietà man and the angel stand up. They are facing the man, the angel behind the pietà man who has now become an angel.

The pietà man screams.

Apparently only he who knows about the scream can hear it.

The man collapses. The man who has become an angel comes up to him. He kneels and cradles the man.

Pietà.

A new man enters. Screams and falls. Pietà.

Yet another new man. Screams, falls, and pietà.

Another man, the scream again, and the fall. Pietà.

Then all the men who have become angels scream. I'm the only one who knows this, and I'm screaming with them.

The angel falls. All the men who have become angels come up to him. They kneel. They cradle the angel.

Pietà.

III

ND more time passed, but no longer was anything as before. Outside, the city began to change, and its men began to change. Faces in the street smiled in a different way. They all have a knowing look, the look of someone who understands something. What do you know? I ask them. We know, they reply, we know. And more.

I no longer dare to look at them. Their eyes don't leave me.

And their words.

Inside me.

Tongues no longer wag in a vacuum (the time is no doubt near when they will no longer need to wag). Life goes on; will it need to go on much longer, this necessary pretence?

As for me, I watch the door, expecting it to open again to let them in.

Perhaps I'm wrong. My door isn't theirs, but I am.

IV

MY door isn't theirs but the truth is they don't care. As if he'd read my thoughts, today's angel comes in through the window, the crafty creature. Without seeing me. So why come here then? He's looking straight ahead and I follow his glance. Suddenly the light makes an opening in my wall. The duty angel collapses on to his knees, as if struck by lightning. A strange habit no doubt; would that appeal to them? The opening disappears, the angel gets up.

Then the light bursts through the wall again, powerful, unbearable. The angel collapses, struck down. The opening disappears, and the angel gets up.

The light bursts through again. I say to myself: let him come in or go out, but the angel collapses once again, struck down. The opening disappears, he gets up.

The opening reappears, he collapses, it disappears, he gets up. Teetering.

For a moment he's on his feet. He throws me a pleading glance. I don't know what to say to him. I want him to be done with it. The opening reappears, the angel rushes towards it, it disappears, he collapses, struck down.

He's no longer moving.

Not the slightest quivering of his wings.

Silence.

What can I do with an angel's body? There's always something you can do with a man's body, but an angel's body?

I open the window and throw it out (there are plenty of them, why worry?)

Then I sit down again and think of other bodies.

V

UNFORTUNATELY I've scarcely any time to think, for very soon a tall skinny angel with dark eyes is in front of me. He tells me what I did is unacceptable, that you don't go throwing an angel out of the window, that it's unheard of, that if I can't look after my angels they won't send me any more of them, they'll look elsewhere, that there are plenty of others who would like to have them, that some people have been waiting for ages, that there are lots of saints and visionaries far more deserving than me, that if they hadn't made a mistake in the first place (so that was it), they would have made sure not to come to my place, but okay, since they were already here they might as well continue, unless I myself wanted to put a stop to it, but then if that was the case I should say so, but certainly not by throwing out the angel as I had done, no joking.

He is all flushed and looks as if he might explode. I say nothing, a little shamefaced. I don't dare say to him that I find these angels rather thoughtless with their clowns' faces, coming in through one window and not wanting to leave the same way. But perhaps he's right after all, and I shouldn't have done it.

I say, yes, I shouldn't have done it, no I won't do it again. Please Sir Angel, please send me some more angels nevertheless, and please don't give me those dark looks.

Then he softens, smiles benignly at me, playfully smooths a wing, tells me okay then for this time, but make sure you don't do it again.

Outside the night is silent.

I watch through the window as he leaves. He politely greets an old gentleman who is sweeping up feathers.

A fly passes by.

I keep quiet.

Are the flies angels?

VI

AFTER waiting for quite a while the new day finally dawns, and my foreboding with it. Will they come back? The skinny angel looked pretty angry yesterday. But he said nevertheless that they'd be back. What if he'd lied to me? If he's changed his mind? If they never came again? Then it would be out of the window for me.

I have a feeling that I can no longer do without them, my angels, my discontented little angels.

They take my mind off things.

And sometimes they look so stupid, so serious. They make me laugh.

Are they ever coming back or are they permanently angry? Whatever, I'm waiting for them.

VII

I was right. They're back. There was I thinking that none of them would come back, and here are so many of them—it serves me right—that I have to move to another room. Now we are all in a great hall. Station or factory? But even here there are too many of them so that they have to leave their wings outside. That obviously doesn't upset them; I have the impression that they're naked. Am I finally going to know the colour of their genitals? (And the smell of their genitals? do angels have a smell?) It seems the question has no importance, and they're laughing at it. Great loud laughter, powerful laughter, resonates in this great hall, makes the walls vibrate. Is that why they all suddenly vanish? My angels disappear and I find myself alone in the vast space, tiny me.

Ah! To make love with an angel, with a thousand angels.

Perhaps next time. I close my eyes.

Now I have something to dream about.

VIII

BUT I didn't dream, I couldn't. Nor sleep. I couldn't sleep either. I tossed and turned, worrying, with that constant worry that they might leave me. What they did yesterday, wasn't that to punish me? To disappear suddenly like that, leaving no trace, no feathers. And me with my arms open to embrace their shadows.

IX

TODAY I won't go out, I won't eat, I won't read, I won't see anybody. Too bad for the outside world. I'll forgo my little tipple at the bar, I'll forgo my window shopping at the bookshop, I'll forgo my walk along roads you can cross without looking, I'll forgo the smell of tarmac. I'm leaving the city outside and I'm sitting inside and waiting. The men in the street have killed the angels in my head. But when they come back I'll set my angels on the men so they can make short work of them.

My angels bark, my angels bite.

My angels wreak their vengeance on those who shoot at them on the wing.

My angels will wreak their vengeance on me.

But I will save my angels from men's spittle. I'll save them from my own stupidity, I'll shelter them from my ignorance, my impotence, my powerlessness.

Now they are mine, for me, inside me.

If I slept, out of my sleep an angel would emerge.

If I spat, out of my spit an angel would emerge.

If I sang—heaven forfend—an angel would emerge from my song.

And from my cries.

And from my tears.

And from other things too.

Yes, I won't go out, won't eat, won't drink. I shall force them to come, my longing will summon them. Hunger and thirst will make me a virgin when they arrive; my absence from others will make them the first today to meet my eye. I certainly owe them that. Or do I not? In any case, I'm waiting.

They will come.

X

TOTALLY calm inside, totally calm outside. Obviously, they haven't come. Such bastards, my angels. But it's my fault too. In order for angels to come, it's a well-known fact that men have to keep quiet. If my angels aren't coming, it's because I talk too much. They need an empty space in my city and inside me. Leave space for them in my voice.

XI

EVENING approaches. Neither men nor cars are to be seen in the streets. Now and then a bell rings in the emptiness. They have abandoned me. I didn't manage to keep them, or to hold them, or to speak to them. So fragile, my angels.

Don't ask them anything.

Don't try to know.

Don't keep seeking rhyme and reason all the time.

Understanding an angel? An angel can't be understood, he can only be observed in silence.

XII

IDIOT that I was, idiot that I am, that I shall always be.

They couldn't not come back since I was waiting for them. I just needed to want them a little bit more, night needed to fall, for them to appear once again in my room in all their glory. I just had to stop getting worked up, play acting, for the benefit of whom, of what? Fear panics at being left alone, fear panics at not facing up to things, and makes you turn your back. Like a puppet that doesn't even scare the crows which perch on his head. I'll always be an idiot. Yet they came back (unless it was the crows?)

Just as I was getting ready to close my eyes, I saw a big rope ladder fall from my ceiling and down it came, a long line of angels looking serious and sad. Having read the story I thought they were coming down to me; but scarcely had the first one put his foot on me than they left again just as quickly, without even leaving me their ladder as a souvenir.

What clowns my angels are—and I'm their red nose, no longer laughing.

With them gone, all is still again, except perhaps the shape beneath my sheets.

XIII

IN the morning however, still in the quiet of the night, someone knocks on the door. I don't move, because if I move all this beneficial stillness will drop away. The smallest gesture, the least breath, and the flavour of the night will melt away, will obscure the memory of my angels. I don't move, and I wait, sure of my victory since they came back, poor acrobats with their clipped wings.

There is a louder knock.

Once, twice.

Then a little angel's head comes in through the window, and draws back quickly (the memory of another angel, another window?) The knocking on the door starts up again, more and more gently, and suddenly the noise stops.

Time.

The door opens quietly. On the threshold is the angel from the window who looks at me hesitantly. I would never have believed that an angel could be shy. We smile at each other, for it seems that is the only thing we can do. Without moving, me from my chair, him from the threshold, we smile at each other. Then he slowly closes the door.

Time.

I can hear him breathing on the outside, myself on the inside. His breathing soothes me. Patiently. Simply. I could easily go back to sleep, a peaceful sleep at last. Then the door opens again. He smiles at me, I respond. And he gently closes the door again.

Time. He is still breathing, still gently. His breath is regular, patient, steadfast. Then the door opens, it starts again. The same thing, three more times.

Then, feeling a little tired, I lie down again, believing nothing has happened. And he, disappointed, goes away too.

That night I don't sleep. I think of him. What should I have done?

The next morning I get up. For a few days my legs hurt. From too much sleep?

XIV

MY angels sleep too, sometimes, or pretend to. Not always where I would want them to.

Coming home this evening I found a very large one of them in my bed, taking up all the room. Sprawling his full length, so long that his feet overlapped the bed. No shame.

Not knowing what to do, not daring to wake him, I sat down, I watched him. I watched him for a long time. He was sleeping like a happy angel, his breathing rapid but regular, and from his mouth I could see thousands of frightened angels emerging. Search as I might I could see no trace of this crowd on or around him. Nothing but his serene, peaceful—I might even say radiant—features.

Tiredly, I waited for him to wake up and restore my bed and my dreams to me. But he seemed happy between my sheets. An hour. Two hours. Then three, then four. At the end of my tether I slid into the bed, pushing him aside as much as I could, pulling the quilt over me, kicking and punching. And he groaned without waking, and even more angels came from his mouth. A cloud of them around us, flying hither and thither. Two or three even burned their wings on my candle.

Then the flow dried up (a dearth of angels, you might say). When everyone had gone and his colleagues had taken off for pastures new (other beds like mine?) he started to move, and got up, still sleeping.

Scarcely had he left when I heard a lot of noise outside the window.

But I didn't care, as long as I could sleep.

And I slept, slept at last, in my turn. But alone.

XV

DID he understand my regrets? Yesterday's angel came back. When I opened the door he was there, in my bed again, breathing out myriads of angels. This time I didn't wait. I slid in next to him.

As he didn't react to my caresses I eventually joined the crowd of his angels. I fled with them. I left him between my sheets for as long as his dream lasted, or mine.

When I came back he had disappeared.

One more lost.

XVI

HOWEVER, another one has settled above my bed.

He has made himself a place in the corner between the wall and the ceiling. Wedged in like a great big spider waiting for its prey. Even though I know that a spider doesn't have wings, I haven't slept the past two nights. I pass the time with my eyes open. I watch him, just in case. He looks at me impassively. What does he want? I've nothing to offer him. My body is empty, what have I to feed it with? I wish he'd go, I wish he'd go, I wish he'd go, oh my angels.

Sometimes his arms move, imperceptibly. They tremble, as if my breath moved the web that they're weaving, invisibly. His large eyes are on me like hideous hands. And his mouth, oh, his mouth.

Is he going to go? The hours pass and he sucks my blood, my bone marrow, my brain.

I close my eyes.

I open them again. He is no longer there. Or is he beneath the sheets? I howl until I see him again. He's just moved to a different corner.

I'm reassured. If I can see him, it means he's at a distance.

His eyes devour me, but my own protect me.

But still, but still, an angel up there, what a pain.

I take my courage in both hands. I stand up, get hold of my slipper—with one blow I crush him.

A small blob of blood mixed with feathers is left in the shadows.

XVII

"DONKEYS can see angels, and that should hardly surprise us."

So was that it, those ears pushing me and falling over my eyes? No longer able to see, my braying finally makes sense. Or not?

XVIII

WHAT are they going to do? Will they finally explain to me what they are waiting for? And me? Do I have to wait for them, really? In any case, previously when I was bored, I was bored – today I strip the feathers off an angel: "I love him, I love him not, I love him a little, I love him a lot. He hates me, he hates me not, he hates me a little, he hates me a lot, he hates me passionately, he hates me placidly. I hate him passionately, methodically if I can. I pull out his feathers a little, a lot, voluptuously—and then I take another one. Waiting for someone or something to come. Angels' petals around me, angels' petals around me and everywhere beneath my feet.

But nothing happens.

Until the shy angel reappears. And I'm on

my chair again, and he's smiling as before. Is he going to start again? Why is he smiling at me? What have I done to him? What good? What ill?

I'm getting tired of my angels (as are others, no doubt).

But now he falls upon me, knocks me over, stuns me and beats me mercilessly. I howl, but a crowd of angels arriving from I don't know where responds to my cries and overpowers me in their turn. They hit me, they scratch me, they bite me. I can feel their teeth. I sense that they're tearing at my flesh. Devouring me like wolves. But that's not all, they're holding onto my legs, the shy angel throws himself between my thighs teeth bared; I howl but he continues, he's dismembering me, swallowing me, consuming me—pitiless. Blood runs from his lips, he licks his chops, spits me out again with a grimace, then smiles, again, but this time beatifically. And I'm thrown back, exposed to the air, parts liberated, scattered over my feet, I'm dripping, empty, I'm coming, I'm weeping, and I suddenly wake up and see my angel still smiling and looking at me from the threshold; he hasn't moved.

Then, satisfied, replete perhaps, he leaves

quietly, gently closing the door, still discreet, still shy. And I close my eyes. Sleep has come back to me. Sleep has come back to me. Sleep has come back to me.

XIX

TODAY—is it an effect of last night?—I witnessed a strange scene. Now they've begun to act. See how they're destroying me from inside.

When I go out (I notice that hasn't been happening for a long time—how lovely to be no longer going out), when I go out then, even in the street, everything seems normal. But when I look at the couples around me they're not properly speaking couples, but rather more like double men. It seems as if they all, in twos, turns their backs to each other and talk to someone in front of them. But in fact they're speaking to the one who's behind their back. You can hear the murmuring of their words, sometimes the voices are raised; you could almost make out the sense. From the quivering shoulders, the trembling voices,

I realise a certain sentence has struck home. But these bodies are not separate. You would think they'd exchanged their hands and their arms rather than their mouths and that they stay linked together without ever facing each other.

I would like to go to help them, but an angel takes my hand and leads me back home. When I turn round they've disappeared. Just men with empty stares remain. Further away an angel passes and smiles at me. I don't care about angels' smiles (oh, why can't they finally leave me alone).

XX

SPEAKING of smiles, I notice they all have the same one. If it's true that men make angels in their own image then my image is pretty ugly. Is that grimace they offer me my own face?

I close my eyes, and here's one beside me.

I close them again, and there are two of them.

I close them again, and there are three.

Close them, and there are four.

Close them, there are five, then six, then seven.

Close again, and close and close and close, and there are a hundred, or a thousand or more, smiling at me, sweetly.

Then I keep my eyes open to stop the flow of them. And as my tears flow, they plunge into them and drown.

Why does their smile stay with me? Let it be gone, let it be gone, let it be gone.

XXI

THIS morning I get up, wash and dress, with my angels and their smile in my head. And I go down to the street again, I have to live—or pretend to. Below the crowds are on the move, and I, unseen, watch them. The postman walks along, the fireman walks along, the tramp walks along, the gardener, the grocer, the whole district as one man (what, men? Are there still some?) They are all walking along. And I see them pass by, disappear, then return, as if all they were doing was circling some undefined axis. Except that on this axis, or not far away, I see there is an angel. A little while ago that might have surprised me. I would have rubbed my eyes, pinched and slapped myself, gone to look. But today I'm no longer surprised. The angel seems to be in his place.

Raising his hands he watches the strange procession pass by, fishmonger, baker, street sweeper, the whole tra-la-la of my crazy city. It lasts for a long time without my finding myself part of their weird ballet. But the angel watches patiently, with his hands raised, and I watch the angel. After a while his arms get heavy, the angel grimaces, his hands are shaking. He drops them; the crowd falls with them, violently. My city, my angels, every day everything falls apart a bit more. And me too, perhaps, soon.

Then the angel raises his arms again.

Slowness, heaviness, pain of the raised hands. The crowd gets back up. And the pain comes back. The arms fall again, the crowd falls too. The angel struggles, poor little angel, raises his arms, raises the crowd.

Then two of the crowd come, sit him on a stone, hold up his arms. Relief.

The crowd turns and comes past, and disappears.

The two from the crowd disappear too.

The arms drop.

The angel is lost.

I approach and sit down. He whispers in my ear a name that I don't understand. We smile at each other, not getting very far. I don't like mysteries.

XXII

SPEAKING of mysteries, what's the name of that other one who I'm in contact with? I kick his shin, he taps me on the shin. I pull his ears, he pulls my ears. I pummel his ribs, he bashes my chest. I twist his neck, he screws my head round. I dislocate his shoulder, he puts my eyes out. I'm no more than a bleeding mass at his feet, he is the blood I'm swimming in.

XXIII

AND don't think he's alone, the one who is eating away at me. All my angels are terrible.

Pitiless.

Thus, how many times since the first one have they woken me during the night, pulling at my feet, threatening me, begging me to get to work. To work for what? To do what? Sleeping, doing nothing, drinking a coffee in a corner by the bar counter or on the gold-coloured table—all that's so good. But they've spoiled the coffee for me, spoiled the coffee maker too sometimes I feel, because I can no longer look at him without seeing angels around him. Terrorist angels. Angels everywhere, angels for everyone, it's exhausting. And no use telling them I'm tired, no use rubbing my eyes to make them understand

I'm tired, they won't leave me in peace. They grab at my quilt, persecute me, I who only dream of that little cosy bed with a still warm sleeping shape. And they, do they have work to do? Do they have evil angels who wake them up and persecute them? Death to the angels.

XXIV

PEACE to my angels, they don't know what they're doing.

It can't be said often enough, they're a strange lot. Here they come looking for me today, with a mysterious air, all smiles. They talk to me of holidays. We'll take you away they say, you'll see, things will change. Follow us. Don't be afraid. Etc., etc. And we go down the stairs—in single file like good little angels. And then they're flying away, the first followed by the second, the second followed by the third, the third followed too, and so on, until the last one lifts me on to his back.

Above us, the clouds; below us, the city. I can see the traffic flowing smoothly, creeping along in clouds of smoke, and pedestrians slowly passing by. Some of them look at the sky to see what the weather's doing; they don't see my angels. How I pity those I see, and how I envy them. We encounter birds who avoid us, apprehensive—fearful of competition. And I follow them, forgetting that I don't know how to fly, since my angels kindly do the flying for me. Indeed, I'm happy to float, between two skies, rolled along by the clouds. They talked to me about holidays. Ah, how I love holidays.

But it all comes to an end and we go back home, taking the staircase as is proper. They let me go back to bed. Between my sheets I feel again the cool of the clouds.

XXV

I find it difficult to tear myself away from the sheets' caress, but a repeated noise wakes me. A sliding sound, then some little tapping sounds; one, two, three; another sliding sound, more taps and so on. I get up and look out of the window.

An angel is playing hopscotch with some children. Concentrating, beneath their serious gaze, he slides between the sky and the earth. One two, he jumps. One two three. One two three four he jumps. Three four five. Legs apart, legs crossed. And the shining eyes of the children who seem to be waiting for him to make a mistake. One two three hell-fire. Laughter.

But the angel starts again.

A second angel approaches and joins the children. He laughs and then takes his turn at the game. One two three. Four five six. Seven eight: lost!

Two other angels join them. They watch, then join in the hopscotch. The marker slides. Eight nine: lost!

Then all my angels come and join in, from the four corners of the city. One two three. Four five six. Seven eight nine. Go to hell!

XXVI

ANOTHER time I wake up, feeling uneasy again. Outside a black angel is coming past. The men all rush over, then immediately stop.

They watch him passing by.

A man comes out of the crowd. He goes up to the black angel and embraces him. Time. They look at each other, then the angel continues on his way and the crowd gets on with its business.

Everything goes blurred, then disappears. The man has gone.

When I go downstairs all is normal. Except me, says the voice of the clown who once was a king.

XXVII

IT'S raining.

I'm scarcely due a visit from my feathered companions, and yet I know that one of them is waiting for me on the other side of the wall. A large very wet angel, whom I'll take in my arms to warm him up. A soaked angel whom I'll dry with my breath, whom I'll dress in my smartest clothes, whom I'll wrap in my dirty sheets. My own angel, whose guardian I'll be (I shall keep him for a few days behind the window bars of my room, or in a drawer, or in a shoe box, or somewhere deep in my foggy brain). Perhaps out of gratitude he'll pass some of his wisdom on to me, who am so stupid?

That will be the moment to send him on his way.

XXVIII

ANOTHER tedious question, believe me: what does an angel dream about? I who hardly dream at all (except about my angels), I'm asking myself that. A mouse dreams about a cat, I about my angels, but what do my angels dream about? If only my angels dreamed about me, that would give me some importance—in my own eyes, of course. But I'm not completely sure of that. No doubt I'm absent from their thoughts, by day as well as night. My angels leave me lonely.

But do they even dream? For they no longer sleep (elsewhere than in my bed). They're there, watching, all the time. They wander the streets in all directions, afraid of being useless. No one here needs them, or just a little. Except me, whom they don't need.

So what keeps them awake is not their usefulness but my misery.

Poor little angels. Poor me. Poor all those who don't have angels, and all those who do. Feathers on feathers.

At least I know that with mine I can always fill up my bolster. That's always it, a pillow full of angels.

XXIX

TODAY, walking along the street, I almost bumped into a crowd of angels. Ten angels, twenty angels, entwined, in front of me.

I avoid them at first, out of prudence, but as I skirt round them I suddenly realise that it's me they're watching, that it's me they're interested in. Perhaps they resent me, I who have done nothing to them. Perhaps too that's what I've done wrong, to not do anything to them.

Their huge mass shakes with laughter. Knowing me, I think they're laughing at me; but as I do in fact know myself, I pull myself together, and pretend to ignore them. But now they really are laughing at me, I was sure of it, all my angels are given to mockery, and cruel and heartless—and what else?

It's so true, I'm certain that in their fracas it's me they're trampling on.

Pulling myself together I run to them, throw myself at them, I want to disband them, tear them apart, so that they'll leave me alone, that they'll stop laughing at me, and go away. And they do go, a flight of angels playing at being afraid fleeing from the naughty child pursuing them.

As they flee one of them drops what? A photo of me, taken where, in what place? Me, looking ridiculous, with giant wings, such huge wings, and me so small.

XXX

THAT photo haunts me. Midget that I am. Fixed like a fly to a dung heap. That said, a fly surrounded by angels is nevertheless better. I see myself wasting away between those wings which don't belong to me. I can't fly of course, nor budge an inch. And there they are, laughing at my starved corpse, entangled in its wings. And, as I die, my body falls to dust and the wings are left alone.

Not even the shape of my body as a link between them. Two brackets—and a great empty space between them.

XXXI

THE photo doesn't leave me, I have fixed it to my chest.

Well, I say fixed, it's to give a better impression. I stuck it with a sticking plaster. It's painful though, with the chest hairs you know. Each to his own tragedy.

I go everywhere with my photo. I carry it everywhere, like a part of me. Now I've stuck my stigmata to my body. My photo and me. Me and my photo. We parade around.

XXXII

WHILST I parade around (since now it would seem that's all I know how to do) I suddenly see again the crowd from the other time, or another which looks like it. They're still looking at me, this time without laughing. So I ignore them. For good. I know perfectly well it's my looking at them that brings them to life, so why would I give it to them now that I have my photo?

But they don't see it that way. Do they want to take back their property, or simply tickle me? They rush upon me, as I did previously upon them. But I don't fly away, and for a good reason. They are well aware that I can't.

What will they do? Where are they taking me, as if in triumph? And the photo—why don't they take it back? I ought to have understood that it was just bait, another one for the person I see in the mirror. They leave me quite naked. Naked, they immerse me in tar. You'd have predicted it, except that I never suspect anything—that's my bad luck, my naivety.

The feathers follow, of course.

And I, poor tarred bird, thrown back onto the riverbank.

XXXIII

TIRED. I'm tired. I'm tired of my angels. That's why I've put them aside. In my cupboard. Locked in. And double locked.

I waited for them to show themselves, those of them anyway who had not voluntarily given up hassling me, I set a trap for them. A well-known lover's ploy. They knock, I open my door and my arms. I set the table and I feed them. Bread, wine and more, as far as perfume sprinkled on their heads. We chat like old colleagues. They tell me what they've seen, those they've "accompanied"— that's their word (I've a cruder one, I admit) before me. That's how I learn that one of them was previously with a Samaritan woman; having fallen from grace he's now been allocated to me, bound to me. Another, changed into a black dog by his master, attached himself to me to expiate, he says, an even blacker sin and for which he can never redeem himself—thank you, I think. They no longer know their names. Four others with them tell me they have no names, but that their own masters are called Kukutiel, Tralaliel, Shazamiel, and Lullabiel, and that they have travelled extensively. With such names I can believe it—who would want them by their side? My own name, what is it? I realise I've forgotten it too. Perhaps it's the alcohol. It doesn't matter, I'm sufficiently in control of myself to continue. After opening my arms to them, my table, my bottles and my heart (they believe; I'm an impostor), I open my bed and a bit more.

Then, yes, I'm jubilant. For at the crucial moment, I imitate thunder at my window.

Afraid, thinking someone is after them, they rush to the wardrobe. It's a stampede. They lose all self-control, pushing, insulting, biting each other, to get more quickly into hiding. And I'm laughing beneath my sheets. Then, when they've calmed down, I close the wardrobe and take the key.

It's in the bag, my angels too as you might say.

They're still there, behind the door. They bang on the door, hammering furiously. They'll soon start howling, you'll see. Is that a way for angels to behave? Let them bang, let them howl, I don't care. They're properly trapped. I'll leave them there for a few days, enough time to forget about them.

They're in no danger. An angel is not alive, doesn't die. A little time off will do them good. They can meditate. And I'll sleep.

XXXIV

I forgot them so completely that when I opened the door they were no longer there.

XXXV

THE peace didn't last. Yesterday two angels wearing hats, whom I didn't know, came to fetch me. Roughly, they told me to get out of bed and get dressed, that I'd been lazing around long enough, that I was a good-for-nothing. I wasn't very happy, I don't like being hassled when I wake up, but they seemed to be getting nasty so I didn't say anything. Without a word I hurried to follow them. Where were we going? They told me I would know soon enough. That this was just a foretaste. In the street people were looking at me, and their angels at their sides were also watching me. What had I done to make all their eyes fix on me like that? I tried in vain to think, but could not remember. Not even a vague memory. All I could find was a clear conscience, white as an angel's wing. Except perhaps the feeling of having slept too much.

The way seemed all the longer as I could not make out where they were taking me. Towards the river, clearly, but why? It's a good while since I used to throw myself into it. Their surly look discouraged questions so I didn't pursue the matter.

When I noticed the Tower I had a vague idea about what they wanted to do, and in fact they pushed me up the staircase – they don't like to use the lift which crumples their wings. Despite my hatred of stairs, I had no choice but to comply. Definitely very irritating.

However, as we climbed they lightened up. They showed me the city, pointed out places. Down there, the Cathedral, there the Institut, there the Palais-Royal, there the Opera House. More roofs than you know what to do with, and smokeless chimneys. They were cheering up, but I was getting tired, missing my eiderdown and pillows. I was telling myself I'd have done better to bring them with me, so I could throw my angels onto them and be done with it. But the harm had been done, there was no point in thinking about it (except that next time I should bring a wardrobe to put them into again).

When we arrived at the top I was out of breath, but they were very jolly. They were laughing so loudly that now everyone was looking at them. Without giving me time to point that out to them, they threw themselves into the void. From there they shouted to me to follow them to try out my wings.

Listening only to my conscience I went down and back to bed.

XXXVI

A voice slips into my head: "The angels mustn't be seen: it's bad luck for angels to be mixed up with men!"

Bad luck for men mixed up with angels.

The speaker whispers in my ear like a crow perching there. Sitting on my shoulder he murmurs and murmurs, words with no meaning, mindless. They echo in my head. My head like a tomb. How did he get out of it? A heavy stone between my two ears. A stone in my belly too, rolling endlessly around, tearing at my entrails. Head and belly, both empty, nothing in them but a loud noise that bangs and hangs and hangs, with no end. A bat with an angel's wings, or the opposite, but it's all the same. And banging on, with no end. Why do there have to be angels in my head, in my belly, in my head, never-ending angels, never-ending angels. I'll make their unceasing voices stop. I'll wake up to get them to stop, I'll wake up. Silence in my head, never-ending silence. And now I wake up, and now in the silence an angel is devouring my belly, he's not in my head, he's on my belly which he's digging into, endlessly, and as I'm howling he looks at me in astonishment, his mouth covered in blood, my blood in his mouth. Look my angel, I'll clean you up. I grab him and twist him and as he madly flaps his wings I twist him harder, twist the hungry angel as if wringing a mop. He squawks. A twisted angel squawking, that's all that comes from my head and from my belly. All that's left for me to do is hang him up and pluck him. What is there beneath an angel's feathers?

XXXVII

I shall not find out as now there is a voice shouting: "Gentlemen of the Court!" and there was I expecting to see a resplendent king coming back (remnants of another dream) when I see a large corpulent angel in a red robe ceremoniously approaching my table whilst two others I didn't see arriving are forcing me to get up. It was a trap, I should have suspected it. They'll get me, finally. Who could seriously have believed in the mop, in the angel on my belly, who, apart me in my naivety? One more trap, and I fell into it.

For the moment the large angel is vituperative, vociferous, belching out more and more words I don't understand. From the way he's staring at me I realise it's me he's talking about. I smile at him, trying to make a good impression; but he just gets angrier.

Being an obliging soul by nature, I start to cry. Furious, he jumps up and down, I keep silent, but now he swells up like a balloon, his face crimson, his wings puffed up with hatred. I lower my gaze, I curl up into a ball, I'd like to disappear, it's no longer funny now. But I hear him suffocating with rage. I look up, he's in a twisted agony which is making his wings flap painfully (so was he the one squawking?) My guardians seize him and carry him off without a word. Leaving me alone.

(I shall have to leave in my turn.)

XXXVIII

DON'T let us rejoice too soon. Alone, but not for long. They have fixed an angel to my backside. One who doesn't leave me this time. A nasty one. To have gone through all that to come to this?

Wherever I go he follows me. If I go out he follows me. If I come home, he's already there. At the café he drinks from my cup. In the street he sits in my shadow (when there's no sun he leaves me alone, but I'm not going to give up winter light just to get rid of him). If I let him he would climb onto my back. He slips in between me and women (and between me and men too, of course, or should I say between me and all my brothers?)

He's everywhere, and I feel as if I'm nowhere. A great discovery, truly. Thank you my angel for this ancient knowledge.

Leave me alone.

XXXIX

LEAVE me alone? I don't know. A bit tired no doubt. I'd like to be alone again. With myself. Or rather with the one that others call me. The one that others think they're greeting when they say hello to me. To be alone like before, without having to justify myself, without having to say why I'm there (nor where I am, nor if I am). A great emptiness like before would reassure me. The nasty one finds me intolerable, in the end. I dare to hope it's reciprocal.

One never pays enough attention to the good luck one has. I was fine before. Dull, and fine. Untroubled and comfortable. Even though I was alone, I could still have a conversation with myself, or if necessary, with those around me. But now. A deafening silence surrounds me and I can't speak.

XL

"GO away," I tell him.
  "No," he says.
  "Why?" I say.
"Because," he says
"That's not an answer."
"No, it's a question," he says.
"And you want my answer?"
"Yes," he says.
"OK, then it's no," I tell him.
"No?"
"No, that's all."
"I'll wait."
And he lies down at my door.
At least this one respects my bed and my bedroom.

XLI

I'D gladly make him my pet, you know. Even if it means following me, at least that would give him a status. That would settle him down. I tried to put a collar on him, but he bit me.

"Go away then."

"No."

"Go away, I tell you."

"No."

"Go away, go away, go away."

"NO."

"Are you going to follow me around like this for long?"

"Yes."

"Go to hell!"

"That would be nice."

PART TWO

I

"**D**EAR ANONYMOUS ANGEL,
"You've been gone again for a while it seems. Have we come to an understanding?

"I'm writing to you and your like, without ever being sure that these words will get to you. We're so far apart, my voice is so weak that I tell myself that it's as if I'm writing to myself, stupidly and hopelessly. A letter-writing narcissus. It's true, I console myself by thinking that your wisdom will be able to mitigate my weakness and that your gaze (like that of some of your winged colleagues) will not be put off by the distance which separates us. Let's say that it beneath your gaze that I'm writing, in the expectation of a small sign you'll make to me with the tip of your immense wing, and that perhaps this time I'll see it properly. For the moment, your silent and peaceful patience overwhelms me.

"So, my dear angel, I'll say to you what I can't say to the others. To start with, I notice that since our first meeting nothing works between me and the world. You fill up my bedroom, and my dreams; outside I see only you. A few human beings, my brothers, try in vain to join me, but it's as if your presence prevents them. The draught from your wings, the splendour of your feathers, frighten them. They look in my direction but can no longer see me. All the photos of me taken since the day you arrived show only an empty shady space, a vague dark shape. So I'd like to be bold enough to beg you to start moving your group somewhere else, for a few days at least, enough time for me to say good-bye. If you're going to eliminate me for good, I'd like at least to warn those who have known me. It wouldn't be very kind to leave them in uncertainty. They won't understand such a suspicious absence. They need me to explain, to tell them the how and the why, and where I'm going and who you are, and all that, and all that, and all that, and all that.

""Therefore it really bothers me, as you might guess, but men are like that. So leave me time to do what I have to do.

"If your gaze should fall upon these lines, thank you in advance.

"Peace be upon you (and upon my poor head)."

II

"DEAR ANGEL,

"You haven't replied to me but I know your answer. Yes I know, though I don't know how I know, that my humble request got to you and that you laughed at it. I'm not angry with you, you know. But allow me to ask you again in possibly vain hope that you will not remain indifferent.

"So, let me come: allow me the time to come. I need—it's only human—to get used to that multitude that you and your colleagues intend to impose on me. Nevermore is a kind word to be only for a poet. Let me have a little more time, just time. I shall be yours body and soul—or just body, since you have already taken away my soul. And my body, what will you do with it? When I myself don't

84

know where to put it, what will you do with it? I'll happily pass it on to you, oh yes, but leave it a little while longer to those who can use it and who love me.

"So I say again, give me the chance to leave the others (those very ones from whom I have been absent for a long time, through unawareness). Let me leave them—then I'll be your man and you'll be my angel.

"Greetings and prosperity to you and yours."

III

"DEAR ANGEL,

"Should I believe you've heard my plea? I seem to have been given some respite, and I hear you less. Am I becoming deaf or are you making less noise? I have the impression that for once I can hear myself live (as before, I mean—as before your arrival). The air around me has its lightness and inconsistency back. I'm not rejoicing at it, believe me, but despite everything I'm breathing more easily. Think of the never-ending responsibility: always having to take care not to swallow an angel (one of those angels who pass, and pass again, with a rustling of their wings), never to sigh for fear of harming you with my breath.

"At the same time, should I admit it to you? I really believe that I'm getting bored. Unless it's the men around me. Have you stopped me knowing how to put up with them? I only look at them now to see who is around them. When I see one walking somewhere, which of you is with him? When I see one dancing here, who is burning his feet? And that other who thinks he's enlightened, which of you has blinded him? Should I only like them now because of you? Save me from that, will you.

"Meanwhile, know that I'm listening, with my ears to the ceiling or my head beneath the sheets.

"All the best to you all. All the best to you."

IV

"DEAR ANGEL,
"I know what you want. I won't do it. I'll use all my strength, all my soul, to resist your appeal. That's my way of obeying you, for I know that your brothers and you will always be able to ensnare me. In your talons (for wings are no longer enough for you, you need talons to go with them) I shall still soon be breathing my last.

"What you want, I won't do it, for it would give me too much pleasure to do it. I have to strengthen myself against you, resist your call, resist the recklessness that you promise. Resist the sweetness of your silence. Resist the violence of your love.

"Humble yet full of pride, I shall be yours completely."

V

"DEAR ANGEL,

"Tell me your name, I'll tell you mine, the one I curse in the night, the one I howl in my dreams, the one who weeps in the tears I don't want to shed.

"Tell me your name, so that I know who you are and who I am, I who call to you in vain.

"Tell me your name, so that I can protect myself. For I know that names are the weapons you hurl against us.

"Is there a word that would deliver me from you? A word that will deliver me from myself? Tell me then. Tell me."

VI

"DEAR ANGEL,
"Once more, nothing is as it should be, and it's my fault. Through talking to you I no longer know what to say to others. Those around me who don't have wings, those I'll have to leave, the words for them are stopped in my mouth—as previously your finger stopped words on the lips of my brothers. Autistic, dumb, or simply silent, it's as you wish, I've lost my voice (and my way amongst my fellow men). I thought I'd found it again, the same strange, exasperated, despairing old voice. But it was nothing but a trap, one of yours no doubt. Just a dream, my voice. Yes, I must have dreamt that I could talk. My voice was not my voice, it was no voice at all. Just a short breath, soon extinguished. Left speechless through crying

out to you with my troubles. Soon what will be left to me?

"Once again I'm missing your inconvenient presence, and hastening my flight by your side.

"Don't leave me any longer. I think I'm ready."

VII

AM I ready? Really ready? I'm not so sure. There are still so many links to be severed, so many memories to be destroyed. And my childhood which won't leave me and which I don't know what to do with, this childhood deep in my body, this seething ulcer that I cherish and that is eating away at me. Do I need to grow up in order to follow you? But my childhood holds me in its grip and stops me growing up to join you. Throbbing, never healing. The sea singing in my ears, the wave beneath the boat, the sand, the smiles of those two whom I cannot name. Eternal solitude when they leave, constantly renewed. Never-ending pain at their absence.

Forgive our childhood as we forgive those who gave birth to us.

I shall have to leave to you everything that is stopping me coming. Or maybe not? Will you allow me take away a little piece of what is greater than I am? A little piece of the tree where I perched to watch you, a little piece of sky from where I watched you without knowing you? A little piece of the grass where I raped you in silence? My angels of despair.

VIII

AND now I've said the word I should have kept to myself. Why speak of childhood when I know that's where the abyss is that's holding me back (the abyss where I'm standing?)

That's when you should have taken me, that's when you should have carried me off. Why did you make me believe that I could get out of it when I know now that this curse on me is for ever. To die at the age of sixteen you were saying. To die so at not to see that. To die so as not to see a large clumsy body forever incapable of taking an angel in its arms. It's no use your telling me it's never too late, it's no small thing to settle your account with a life you shouldn't have lived. You'll learn it to your cost, I'll respond vaguely, you who lurk with impunity in my head and in my room.

IX

ANGEL,
    I know what's left for me to do.
    I shall do it.
I shall do it.
I'm doing it.
—And in one go, one single go

It hurts less than I expected. Have I lost the ability to suffer now?

I am freed from the thought of a future.

Will my blood be sufficient to fertilise the earth beneath my feet? At the point where I am—where I am, yes, really—understanding is hardly important to me. It feels so good to just go along with the evidence.

Now I'm ready. Really ready.

Will you come? I'm waiting for you.

X

ANGEL,
I've waited for so long, so long, so long. Imagine, I believed you wouldn't come again. That's all I needed. I'm unpardonable, but you have pardoned me. You took me by the hand and I took my suitcase. Nothing in my suitcase but a teddy bear and red spectacles (you never know, they might come in useful). We went down the familiar staircase, without a glance into my room—my door, my window, my wardrobe and my bed, all the places you visited (before you settled more deeply into my soul). Neither remorse, nor regrets, nor tears will come to encumber my journey. I understood that from your face, reflecting my expression, peaceful, softened, in fact, returned to its old self. For a moment I thought: how long will

it last? But then I understood that that was just an old idea, a residue which was fading, leaving my thoughts for ever.

Now I'm walking calmly at your side. I have certainty, which I would have gained by resisting you. It is not good to give in to your angels, but it's worse not to give in to them.

XI

I'M walking at your side but our footprints vanish straight away in the snow.—Why the snow?—So my path can be traced.—But since the traces have disappeared?—Go and find out, ask them. I only know that it's snowing and that a voice behind me is calling me and then fading away.

We walk together, you and I. You're unconcerned, I'm not. I'm afraid, just a little. I would like you to talk to me but you keep obstinately quiet. If you would help me, that would be good. My suitcase weighs a ton. But you're rushing on ahead. I could believe that I'm no longer of interest to you. Too bad, I'm walking along, it was you who wanted it, you who told me to. I walk and I sink slowly into the snow, a little bit more with each step. All this whiteness. All this whiteness. Like an advert for washing powder. But the time for adverts has passed; I'm pressing on as obstinately as you're keeping quiet. Besides, if you talked to me now I would no longer hear you.

I leave my suitcase behind.

And my teddy bear.

I put on my glasses but I can no longer see you.

All this whiteness.

All this whiteness.

Go in front, I'm following you. Go on. I'm still coming. With or without you. One step after the other, in this whiteness which is sucking me in. Go on, I'm coming.

All this whiteness.

All this whiteness.

I'm here.

Where are you?

A PARTIAL LIST OF SNUGGLY BOOKS

JULES JANIN *The Dead Donkey and the Guillotined Woman*
GUSTAVE KAHN *The Mad King*
MARIE KRYSINSKA *The Path of Amour*
BERNARD LAZARE *The Mirror of Legends*
BERNARD LAZARE *The Torch-Bearers*
MAURICE LEVEL *The Shadow*
JEAN LORRAIN *Errant Vice*
JEAN LORRAIN *Fards and Poisons*
JEAN LORRAIN *Masks in the Tapestry*
JEAN LORRAIN *Monsieur de Bougrelon and Other Stories*
JEAN LORRAIN *Nightmares of an Ether-Drinker*
JEAN LORRAIN *The Soul-Drinker and Other Decadent Fantasies*
GEORGES DE LYS *An Idyll in Sodom*
GEORGES DE LYS *Penthesilea*
ARTHUR MACHEN *N*
ARTHUR MACHEN *Ornaments in Jade*
CAMILLE MAUCLAIR *The Frail Soul and Other Stories*
CATULLE MENDÈS *Bluebirds*
CATULLE MENDÈS *For Reading in the Bath*
CATULLE MENDÈS *Mephistophela*
ÉPHRAÏM MIKHAËL *Halyartes and Other Poems in Prose*
LUIS DE MIRANDA *Who Killed the Poet?*
OCTAVE MIRBEAU *The Death of Balzac*
CHARLES MORICE *Babels, Balloons and Innocent Eyes*
GABRIEL MOUREY *Monada*
DAMIAN MURPHY *Daughters of Apostasy*
KRISTINE ONG MUSLIM *Butterfly Dream*
OSSIT *Ilse*
CHARLES NODIER *Outlaws and Sorrows*
HERSH DOVID NOMBERG *A Cheerful Soul and Other Stories*
PHILOTHÉE O'NEDDY *The Enchanted Ring*
GEORGES DE PEYREBRUNE *A Decadent Woman*
HÉLÈNE PICARD *Sabbat*
URSULA PFLUG *Down From*
JEAN PRINTEMPS *Whimsical Tales*
JEREMY REED *When a Girl Loves a Girl*
ADOLPHE RETTÉ *Misty Thule*
JEAN RICHEPIN *The Bull-Man and the Grasshopper*
DAVID RIX *A Blast of Hunters*
FREDERICK ROLFE (Baron Corvo) *Amico di Sandro*